Travel to Maurice's World!

Maurice's World is your passport to adventure—online. Explore other books in the *Maurice's Valises* series. Make friends from all over the world. Earn moral badges and collect treasures from Maurice's travels. Create your own Moral Scrolls and play fun games. Plus, stamp your virtual passport using the special code below. And there's more to come soon, including a valise hunt!

Visit mauricesvalises.com

YOUR SPECIAL CODE
IS **FRIEND**

ISBN: 9789491613098-51695

MOUSE PRINTS PRESS
Prinsengracht 1053-S Boot
1017 JE Amsterdam Netherlands

Maurice's Valises

Moral Tails in an Immoral World

Book III: Casablanca

By J.S. Friedman

Illustrations by Chris Beatrice

"We want a story…we want a story…we want a story…" chanted Grandpa Maurice's ninety-eight grandmice plus their assorted forest friends.

"What was that? Did you say you want a story? I don't have any stories," teased Grandpa Maurice.

"Grandpa!!!"

"Well, if you put it that way, maybe I could come up with something. But call me Maurice," he said.

Then he sat himself down in his favorite storytelling chair.

In his favorite storytelling place—in his living room.

Deep in the woods, in the base of an old sycamore tree.

A fire crackled in the fireplace.

A winter's wind wailed outside.

And a new snowfall danced and swept the old snow clean and white.

Maurice, as always, was prepared to tell one of his famous traveling tales.

Behind him, reaching
all the way to the ceiling,
stood a stack of old,
worn valises.

Each piece of luggage had a label on it and was covered with stickers from wherever it had been.

Maurice and his valises had traveled to many different places during his long, long life.

When everyone was settled in, Tiny, the littlest grandmouse, asked, "Can I pick the story Maurice?" Without even waiting for a reply, he continued, "the one on the tippety-top, what does it say, Cabalaska?"

With a chuckle Maurice said, "Casablanca.
Ahhh... Yes, of course."

Maurice stood and reached up high to the old weathered valise.

But he was too short.

So he got out his step stool—half a walnut shell—and stood on the tips of his paws until he was just able to take it down.

Before he opened it, he brushed off a layer of dust which, of course, made him sneeze.

"Achoo!"

When Maurice opened the valise, out spilled a Moral Scroll, a small length of rope, some maps, and a burnoose.

PAW NOTES

A Moral Scroll is a paper with a wise saying written on it. The saying is the lesson learned from a particular traveling tale.

A burnoose is a robe with a hood used by people who live in the desert to protect themselves from the sun.

Maurice wrapped himself in the burnoose, fiddled with his woolly muffler (to keep his storytelling neck warm and snuggly), then settled back into his cushy chair and began.

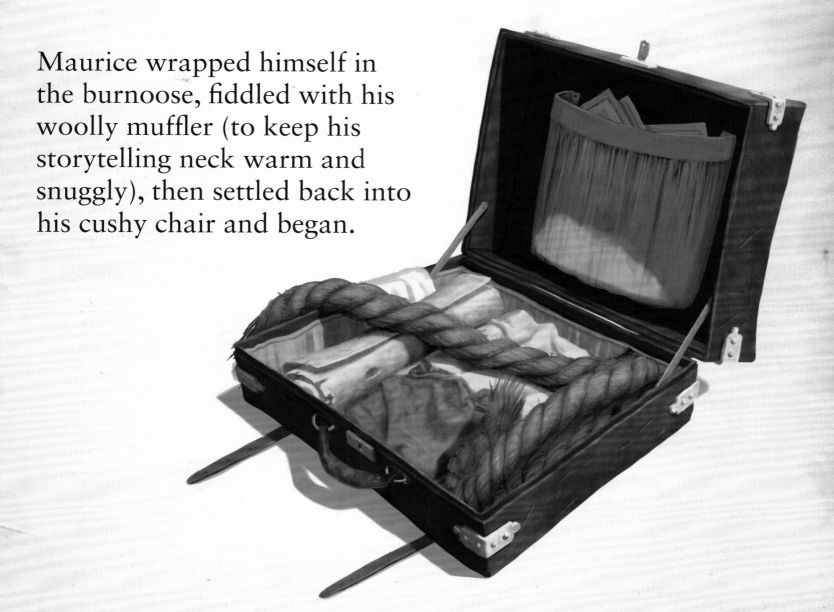

"When I was a young mouse, about as old as some of you, I traveled on an old wooden cargo ship bound for Casablanca, Morocco.

Naturally, I chose to ride below deck in the storage section, where there was plenty of food and room to sleep.

The upper deck was crowded with passengers, but below, that was a different story."

"Below, there were all sorts of boxes and bags filled with food and supplies. There was even a section for animals."

"That's where I met Cecil.

I spotted him right away. Hard to miss a sad-looking camel wearing spectacles on his nose. Even if he was tied to a post, way, way back in a dark corner all alone.

Always ready to eat, I went over to see if there was any food the camel might have dropped.

When I reached him, I saw why he looked so sad. He had wrapped himself around the post so tightly he couldn't reach his food or water."

"I ran up to the post, carrying my valise (this very one), and sat on the rope that held him in place.

I looked into his face and said,
'Hi there, I'm Maurice. Need some help with this rope?'

Cecil looked down through his glasses, with his sad expression, and said, 'Hello, I'm Cecil, but how's a little mouse like you going to help a big camel like me?'"

"At that exact moment, before I could answer, there was a loud crashing sound and the boat shook. I almost fell off the rope.

Above us, people on deck started rushing around and yelling, 'We've struck a rock!'

Suddenly, water began to fill the storage area."

"I heard people shouting instructions to each other about getting into the lifeboats.

But I didn't hear a word about Cecil. Why, nobody even thought about the camel in the hold of the ship.

I looked down at the floor and saw the water beginning to creep up Cecil's legs. Without giving it another thought, I began to nibble through the rope that held him.

The faster the water rose, the faster I nibbled. By the time I finished chewing the last strand of rope, my jaws ached."

"Cecil was able to pull his head away from the post.
He was free.

He looked down his nose at me and said, 'You have saved my life, little Maurice the mouse, and I will be forever grateful. But for now, let's get outta here!'

With that, he kicked a mighty kick against the side of the boat and made a hole large enough to wriggle through—even with his big camel hump."

"I clung to my valise and, using the small piece of rope still attached to Cecil, I swung myself up, scampered over his head, and perched myself on his hump."

"Once we made it out of the hole of the ship and into the water, I could see land in the distance.

I could see palm trees and sand stretching in both directions.

I could see lifeboats filled with people making for shore ahead of us.

And though camels are not known for their swimming, I could see Cecil's strong legs kicking as he camel-paddled toward land.

We were in the water for a very long time.

Waves beat against Cecil, splashing over us. But I held on as Cecil powerfully paddled on."

"When his feet finally touched ground, Cecil staggered to shore, flopped down and spilled me onto the sand.

Exhausted, he immediately closed his eyes.

He flapped his lips and out came a giant camel snore.

Then another.

And another. Until the steady flap/snore…flap/snore… flap/snore made me close my eyes.

Night fell and we both slept."

"The next morning,
I woke to see the shore
covered with debris
from the ship.

Lots of boxes.
Lots of bags.
But no Cecil.

The only sign of my
new friend was a
set of camel tracks
leading out into the desert."

"The sun grew so hot I needed to protect myself.

On the beach, I found some white cloth, fastened it around my head and let the rest cover my body. (I made this very burnoose I'm wearing now.)

Amazingly, I found my valise.

I found food."

"And, as I sat there thinking what I should do next, I found myself hearing the familiar, gentle voice of the Muse of Mice whisper, 'Follow your path.'

Taking courage from these words, I took my valise and began to follow the camel's tracks in search of Cecil.

Months later, I still hadn't found Cecil, but I had found myself a group of new mouse friends."

PAW NOTE

The Muse of Mice is the spiritual protector and guide of Maurice since birth.

"One afternoon, we were in the desert, armed with maps of all the watering holes, trudging toward an oasis.

On the horizon, we saw the tops of green palm trees swaying against the bright blue sky. But behind us we felt the wind picking up and the sands beginning to blow."

"We kept going until we reached the oasis. The sky had already turned dark. A storm was near.

Hurriedly, we drank water from the oasis, then huddled together in our little tent to wait out the storm.

We didn't know it, but at that same moment, another caravan of travelers was making its way to the same oasis."

"Driven there by the sand storm, a convoy of camels with heavy loads finally reached the oasis and settled down to wait out the weather.

The fury of the winds swelled, the palms swayed to and fro, and the howling sounds hurt our ears."

"Suddenly, a giant palm was uprooted and crashed down on top of our tent. We were practically squished under the weight.

It was hard to breathe. And we began to fear for our lives.

I began to yell, 'Help, help!' I hoped for help from the Muse, but how was she going to hear me over the wailing winds?

Just as it seemed all hope was lost,
the weight was lifted."

"Then, a big nose poked itself under our flattened tent. And the nose held a pair of eyeglasses."

"I realized I knew that nose. I knew those eyeglasses. It was my old friend Cecil!

He was one of the camels in the other caravan. He had heard my cries and come to our rescue.

'My friend,' he said. 'I have never forgotten how you saved my life. Now, at last, I am so happy to be able to return the favor.'"

"'Hooray,' yelled my mouse friends.

'Hooray,' I yelled and hugged Cecil.

I climbed up his head and settled in by his soft, furry ear. Cecil told me that he had been recaptured and taken away the very same night after our escape from the ship."

"We talked and talked—I must have almost talked his ear off because it began to droop. We had so many desert adventures to share, we never went to sleep.

By dawn the skies were calm and clear."

"Both our groups got ready to leave. Cecil and I said our goodbyes. I watched through my mouse tears as Cecil's camel caravan disappeared over the horizon."

"Even though I was sad to see him leave, I was happy that
I had such a friend, a friendship I could count on for life.
And that meant so much to me that my sadness went away."

The End

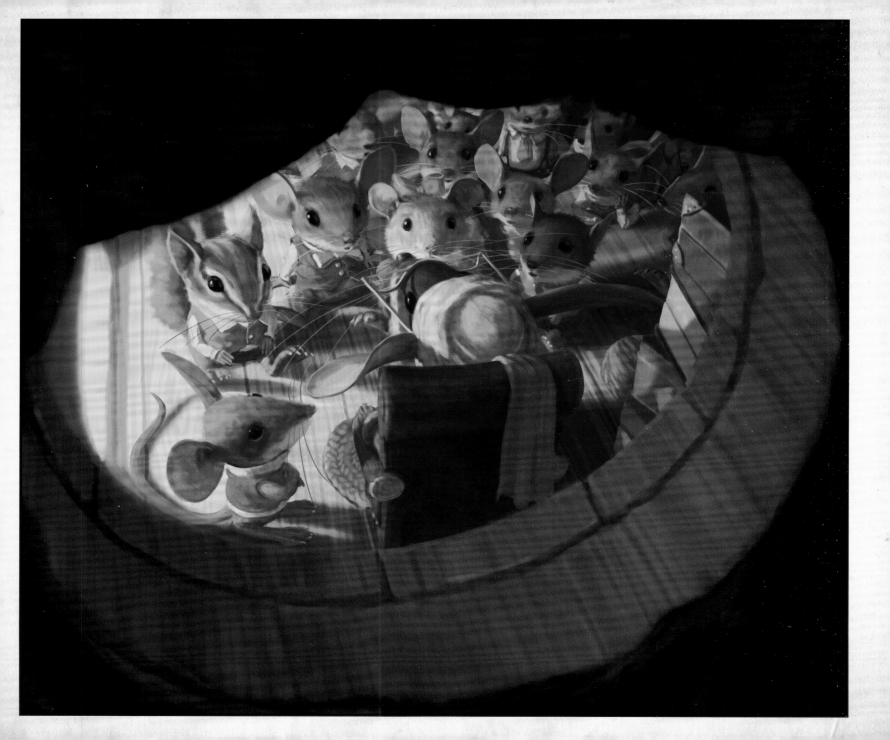

Silence filled the room.

Then Tiny, who had picked the Casablanca story, sniffled back a tear and asked what the Moral Scroll said.

Maurice slowly unrolled the paper. It had been stored for so long it was yellow and full of so many holes it looked like Swiss cheese.

It had words written in neat mouse type. Maurice turned it around for all to see as he read it out loud:

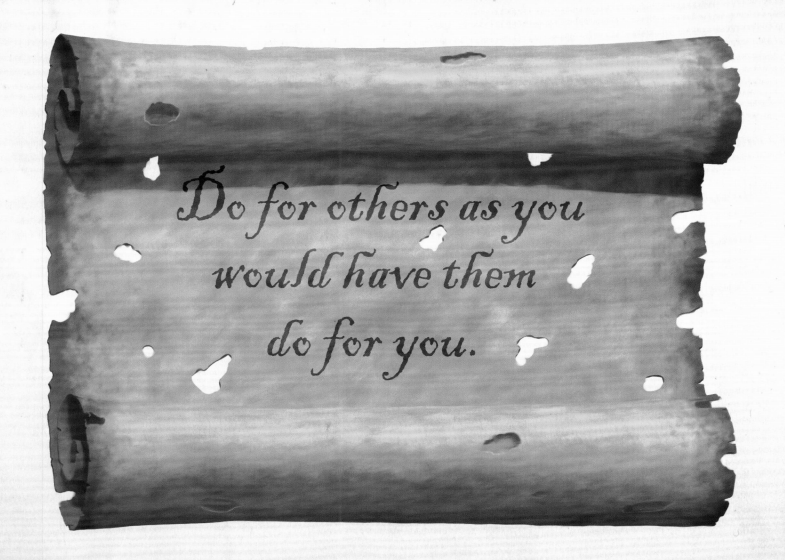

Do for others as you
would have them
do for you.

It took several minutes for the little listeners to whisper among themselves as they thought about the meaning of this.

By the time they looked back at Maurice, the eyes of the elderly mouse had closed, and he was asleep in his comfy chair.

And believe it or not, Maurice flapped his lips and out came a Cecil-the-camel snore.

Then another.

And another.

And another…and…another…

The end, again.
(*But more to come…*)

"Never impose on others what you would not choose for yourself."

–*Confucius*

Confucius (551-479 BC) was a Chinese philosopher whose principles are still respected today. This quote is often referred to as *the Golden Rule*. The Golden Rule is an ethical principle that's found in the teachings of many religions and ancient civilizations.

Acknowledgements

My special thanks to SolDesign for all their artistic input and technical know-how in the creation of this book. To Stephanie Arnold for her unwavering support and crucial editorial contributions. To Joe Landry for his Salzburg friendship and guidance. To my wife and family for all their help. And to Chris Beatrice, for his illustrations and vision and believing that Maurice is a special mouse.

Welcome,

In The Beginning, I traveled New Zealand and in *The Micetro of Moscow*, I journeyed to Russia. And, in *Casablanca* my voyage led me to a great adventure in Morocco. I hope you've enjoyed following me on my adventures so far but like I always say, there's more to come! There is so much more I have to share with you. Still to come in the *Maurice's Valises* series: I explore Germany, the United States, Switzerland, Egypt, Hungary, Thailand and Peru – and learn new moral lessons everywhere I go. What I've seen, you can see. What I've learned, you can learn.

We are all part of a big world – be part of mine! Visit mauricesvalises.com and join Maurice's World. Make friends, play games and learn about the small things you can do to make a big change. I'll see you there!

 –Maurice

DRAW ON ME

DRAW ON ME